Victor Hugo's
The Hunchback of Notre Dame

It was the sixth day of January and all the church bells in Paris had been ringing since dawn, for it was Twelfth Night.

Today the whole city would celebrate the 'Feast of Fools'.

There would be plays and bonfires and maypole dancing. Every square and street was full of musicians and dancers, acrobats and jugglers ready to perform the whole day long, and far into the night.

No one would work on the Feast of Fools day. Instead people could forget their chores, shut up their shops, leave their homes, and join the merry crowd that pushed their way through Paris.

here were many visitors to the city that day. People along the roads leading to Paris had walked all night. Each one wanting to be through the city gates at dawn, so that not one single moment of the day's celebrations would be missed.

Everyone was made welcome - everyone, that is, but the gypsies. Armed soldiers turned them away at the gate, threatening to arrest them if they tried to return.

In those dark days, gypsies were not welcome anywhere. They had to travel great distances, rarely stopping and never making a home for themselves.

However, one gypsy did manage to give the King's guards the slip and enter the city. She was Esmeralda, a beautiful young dancer, along with her beloved pet goat, Djali. In next to no time the two friends were being pushed along by the excited crowd.

In the middle of one of the main city squares was a high platform - a stage,

ready for a play. The people gathered there were already becoming bored with waiting.

"Get on with it!" cried some of the young lads in the crowd.

"Why are we waiting?" yelled Jehan Frollo, the boldest of them all. He threw a stone to attract the main actor's attention, but it flew straight past and crashed through a stained glass window of the cathedral.

ou'd better watch out!" laughed the actor, Gringoire. "Your big brother has just arrived to watch my play."

Jehan's older brother, Monsieur Claude Frollo was one of the most feared men in Paris. He was a powerful man in the church, and was close to the king. His young brother Jehan was probably the only person who was not afraid of him.

"Look at my saintly brother!" laughed Jehan. "With his beetle brows and codfish eyes, and a face like a thunder-cloud!" This made the crowd laugh out loud. "I can see the family resemblance" yelled Gringoire. "He looks just like you. Now let's get on with my play!"

All of a sudden, one of the many ragged beggars jumped onto the stage and held out his hat. The crowd began to cheer and clap, to stamp their feet, and throw coins. This beggar was Clopin, who was very well known in Paris.

It seemed that nobody had time to listen to Gringoire's play! Everyone just wanted to get on with the fun! So poor Gringoire was left standing in the middle of the stage talking to himself.

"As this is the 'Feast of Fools'," shouted Clopin, trying hard to be heard, "we must choose a King of Fools! The ugliest man, or woman here today, shall wear the crown!"

Immediately people began making the ugliest faces they could in an effort to be crowned King.

Then, without warning, a dwarf-like figure appeared, with a hunchback and a monstrous head. He sprang into the crowd.

"It's Quasimodo, the hunchback of Notre Dame!" the people gasped in horror, as they backed away.

uasimodo is my brother's bell-ringer in the cathedral," Jehan told the crowd. "He found Quasimodo abandoned in the cathedral twenty-five years ago. He was just a baby. That poor creature has lived in the bell-tower all his life because my evil brother told him that he was too ugly to be seen. He has been there so long that the bells have made him deaf!"

"Then he will make the perfect King of Fools," laughed Clopin. "For he is certainly the ugliest person I have ever set eyes on!"

The people roared with laughter and crowded around Quasimodo to put a crown on his head, and a cloak on his back. Then they carried him shoulder high through the streets.

Within minutes, Monsieur Claude Frollo rode out into the crowd, his face black with anger. He snatched the Fool's crown from Quasimodo's head.

"Get back to the bell-tower," he ordered the hunchback.

The crowd were losing interest in their King of Fools and many had rushed off to see Esmeralda, the gypsy girl, dancing in the square.

Gringoire the actor had joined them. He soon became enchanted by the beautiful girl as she whirled and twirled to the rhythm of her tambourine. Her little companion Djali, the goat, also delighted everyone with his clever tricks.

t was getting late. The 'Feast of Fools' was coming to an end, and the dark streets became empty as people made their way home to bed.

Gringoire was feeling tired, cold and hungry. He had nowhere to stay for the night, so he followed Esmeralda and Djali.

'Maybe they know where to find food and shelter,' he thought.

Then suddenly, an odd-shaped figure leapt out of a doorway and grabbed Esmeralda. He threw her over his shoulder.

The terrified girl screamed as loudly as she could and struggled to get away. She made such a noise she attracted the King's guards.

With a great clattering of hooves, a horseman galloped down the street and rescued the gypsy girl from the stranger.

Her rescuer was none other than Phoebus, Captain of the Guard! He took Esmeralda into his arms, and Esmeralda fell in love with him at once. But then so did every young girl in Paris who saw him, because he was so dashing and handsome.

The burly men of the King's Guard had quite a struggle to overpower the mysterious person who had tried to kidnap Esmeralda. It was the hunchback of Notre Dame whom the soldiers arrested that night, and threw into prison!

hen Gringoire looked around him, Esmeralda and her goat were nowhere to be seen. The soldiers had marched off and Gringoire was all alone in a dark area of the city he did not know.

Out of the darkness, and without a sound, all the beggars and thieves of Paris appeared, or so it seemed to Gringoire.

"No strangers are allowed here" cried a familiar voice. "We generally hang anyone who is not a thief or a beggar, for this is our part of the city - The Court of Miracles!"

The voice belonged to Clopin, the beggar who had interrupted Gringoire's play that morning. But he looked very different now!

"I am the King of the Beggars" announced Clopin, very grandly. "My word is law here! Hang him!"

"Don't hang him yet" cackled one of the women. "Let him take the test first"

The test looked quite simple. If Gringoire could take a purse from the pocket of a coat covered in bells, without making a sound, he would not hang!

ow the beggars laughed when poor Gringoire tried! As soon as he touched the coat, every bell began to jingle!

"Hang him" screamed the beggars.

"Wait!" roared Clopin. "We have another custom. If one of the girls will offer to marry you, you can stay with us."

Then, as if by magic, Esmeralda appeared, with Djali. They had been made very welcome a little earlier by the beggars.

"I will marry this poor man if it will save his life" whispered the girl.

And so, there and then, Esmeralda and Gringoire were married.

"I like you very much" Esmeralda told Gringoire, "but I have lost my heart to the handsome Captain Phoebus." She slipped away into the darkness.

The next morning, Quasimodo was brought before a cruel Judge, who without a second thought, sentenced the poor hunchback to an hour in the stocks.

A crowd soon gathered, and they laughed and jeered at Quasimodo.

Only one person took pity on him and brought him a drink of cold water. It was Esmeralda.

This made Quasimodo very happy, for no one had ever shown him such kindness before.

When the hour was up, and he was released, Quasimodo almost danced across the square back to Notre Dame. He quickly climbed up into his bell-tower and rang the cathedral bells with joy.

inter came to an end, and spring arrived in Paris. Esmeralda, Djali and Gringoire stayed with the beggars in their hiding place, the Court of Miracles.

Early one spring evening, a party was being held in a grand house opposite the Notre Dame cathedral. The dashing Captain Phoebus was on the balcony, laughing and talking to all the girls as usual. He suddenly spotted Esmeralda in the square below.

"Come up and dance for the guests, Esmeralda," he called to her.

Esmeralda agreed at once, for she had lost her heart to the handsome Phoebus and longed to see him again.

But someone else was watching Esmeralda. It was Monsieur Frollo, standing at the top of one of the towers of Notre Dame, his face dark with jealousy.

While Esmeralda danced, Phoebus flirted with every pretty girl in the room.

'I think every woman in Paris must be in love with Phoebus' thought Esmeralda, gazing at him, as she whirled across the floor.

But a terrible thing was about to happen.

After the party, Captain Phoebus walked Esmeralda out into the dark square.

A hand holding a dagger suddenly appeared from out of the shadows, stabbing towards Phoebus.

Before the terrified girl could cry out, Phoebus fell to the ground - stabbed and bleeding!

Poor Esmeralda fainted, and when she opened her eyes again, she was surrounded by soldiers. People were shouting, "The gypsy girl has killed Captain Phoebus!"

smeralda was immediately arrested and put into prison. Worst of all she was sentenced to hang for murder!

'It must be a mistake!' she thought.

Esmeralda was on the scaffold and about to die, when a remarkable thing happened. Quasimodo the hunchback climbed down the front of the cathedral, knotted a rope around one of the pillars and swung across the square. He rescued Esmeralda in the twinkling of an eye!

Then he ran with her to the steps of Notre Dame. The crowd gasped in amazement as he lifted her above his head, and cried "Sanctuary!"

He then took her into the cathedral, where she would be safe as long as she stayed within its walls.

"Why did you rescue me?" asked Esmeralda as she gazed at Quasimodo.

"You brought me a drink when I was in the stocks. You were the first person to be kind to me, and not treat me like a monster," replied the hunchback, with a tear in his eye. "And that night when I tried to carry you off, I never meant to do you any harm. My guardian, Monsieur Claude Frollo ordered me to do it"

Just then Djali trotted through the door, having climbed the hundreds of steps that led up to the bell-tower. He was with his mistress again.

Days passed and Quasimodo continued to take care of Esmeralda. He brought her food and water, and often freshly picked flowers.

Sometimes Quasimodo would ring the bells just for Esmeralda, but after a while she begged him to stop.

"They're so loud," she said. "It's no wonder you're deaf!"

ack at the Court of Miracles, the beggars were getting more anxious about Esmeralda as the days went by.

"My poor Esmeralda still can't leave the cathedral" sighed Gringoire, "I've heard that the King's soldiers are going to arrest her within three days, in spite of the sanctuary of the cathedral".

"We must get her out at once!" cried Clopin, as he handed out weapons to everyone. "We march on the cathedral in one hour."

Later, as he looked from the bell-tower, Quasimodo saw the great crowd of people surging towards the cathedral.

Clopin hammered on the cathedral doors with his cudgel. "We are here to rescue Esmeralda and to take her to safety" he shouted with all his might.

But as Quasimodo was deaf, he could not know what Clopin was saying. He thought the crowd had come to kill Esmeralda. Before the beggars had time to break down the great doors, the hunchback began throwing huge stones and beams from the roof of the cathedral.

A troop of the King's Guard came riding into the square.

"Look" cried Esmeralda, "There is Captain Phoebus! He's alive! He was not murdered after all"

Clopin, Gringoire, and all the people in the crowd saw that it was indeed Phoebus.

"People of Paris" yelled Clopin at the top of his voice. "Phoebus is alive! Esmeralda is not guilty of murder! She must be set free at once!"

ery slowly Quasimodo led Esmeralda down from the bell-tower. He pushed open the great doors of Notre Dame and the strange couple stepped out into the square.

How the crowd roared and cheered.

Then Captain Phoebus explained how he had recovered from his wound very quickly, but had then been sent to another part of France with his soldiers.

"I have only returned to Paris this very day, just in time to save you," he smiled at Esmeralda, with a twinkle in his eye.

"You didn't save me" said Esmeralda, gently taking the hunchback's hand, "Quasimodo did!"

Then Esmeralda turned to smile at Gringoire.

"I know now that I don't really love Phoebus, and he has never loved me, I promise to love you Gringoire, for ever and ever."

The crowd cheered as if they would never stop. They cheered Captain Phoebus who by now was standing with several giggling girls. They cheered Clopin, King of the Beggars. But they saved the biggest and loudest cheer of all for Quasimodo, who rang the bells of Notre Dame louder than he had ever rung them before.